Christmas Time

The Snow Queen

There were once two best friends, Gerda and Kay. They told each other everything, and everywhere they went, they went together.

"Hello Kay!"

Gerda and Kay loved playing outside – in spring, in summer and in autumn.

"Hello Gerda!"

But Winter was their favourite season. Grandmother told the best stories during the cold evenings. One night, the story was about the Snow Queen.

"The Snow Queen lives in a huge snow palace,"
said Grandmother. "Her enchanted snow settles deep
in your heart, so you forget who you are."

That night, Kay couldn't
sleep. He kept thinking
about the Snow Queen.
He opened his window
to peer down at
the icy street.

In that moment, the Snow Queen threw down a speck of enchanted snow and captured Kay's heart.

The next day, Kay didn't **feel himself**. He was mean to Gerda, shouted at his mother and didn't play nicely with anyone.

As each day passed, Kay seemed to find new ways to be horrible. The Snow Queen's enchantment was working its magic.

Then, one morning as Kay played alone, a huge, SPARKLING sleigh appeared over the hill.

The Snow Queen had come to snatch Kay away.

When Gerda came
to look for him,
Kay was gone.
Gerda searched
everywhere but Kay
wasn't in the village
any more.

Gerda was certain the Snow Queen had stolen Kay away. So, she left the village to search for him.

Kaaa   kaaa!

After many miles,
Gerda met a raven.
"I've seen your friend,"
said the raven.

"He's with the Snow
Queen at her palace."

Gerda followed the raven deep into a forest.
Suddenly robbers appeared. Thinking her rich,
they stole Gerda's things, and bundled
her into a cart.

They took Gerda to their house and locked her in a barn.

A little robber girl lived there too, and she showed Gerda all the animals she looked after.

Gerda told the robber girl about her search for Kay. That night, the girl helped Gerda escape so she could continue her journey.

The robber girl gave Gerda her favourite reindeer to ride, and a warm cloak to wear.

"My reindeer will show you the way to the Snow Palace," said the girl.

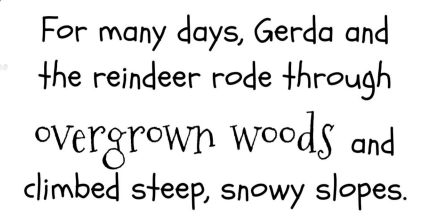

For many days, Gerda and
the reindeer rode through
overgrown woods and
climbed steep, snowy slopes.

At last, frozen and exhausted, Gerda arrived at the *magnificent* Snow Palace.

Gerda felt very scared, but she loved and missed Kay very much. She pushed open the doors to the Snow Palace and went inside.

Sitting on the frozen floor in the middle of an icy room was Kay. He was staring into space, and didn't recognize Gerda at all!

"Oh Kay," cried Gerda dropping to her knees, "how can I help you?" But Kay didn't move. Exhausted, Gerda curled up by her friend and cried herself to sleep.

As Gerda slept, her tears WARMED Kay's hands. The ice began to melt and Gerda's love for Kay thawed the enchanted snow!

Suddenly, Gerda felt Kay hug her tightly.

"I remember you," he said, and the best friends ran laughing from the melting Snow Palace.